Angelina Ballerina

Illustrations by Helen Craig   Story by Katharine Holabird

Clarkson N. Potter, Inc./Publishers

More than anything else in the world, Angelina loved to dance. She danced all the time and she danced everywhere, and often she was so busy dancing that she forgot about the other things she was supposed to be doing.

Text © 1983 by Katharine Holabird
Illustrations © 1983 by Helen Craig
All rights reserved.
Published in the United States of America by Clarkson N. Potter Inc.,
a Random House Company, distributed by Crown Publishers Inc.,
201 East 50th Street, New York, New York 10022
First published in Great Britain by Aurum Press Ltd.
This edition first published in Great Britain by ABC
Manufactured in Singapore

Library of Congress Cataloguing in Publication Data
Craig, Helen.
Angelina ballerina.
Summary: A pretty little mouse wants to become a
ballerina more than anything else in the world.
[1. Ballet-dancing—Fiction. 2. Mice—Fiction]
I. Holabird, Katharine. II. Title.
PZ7.C84418An 1983 [E] 83-8233
ISBN 0-517-57668-6
10 9 8 7 6 5 4 3 2

Angelina's mother was always calling her, "Angelina, it's time to straighten up your room now," or "Please get ready for school now, Angelina." But Angelina never wanted to go to school. She never wanted to do anything but dance.

One night Angelina even danced in her dreams, and when she woke up in the morning, she knew that she was going to be a real ballerina some day.

When Mrs Mouseling called Angelina for breakfast,
Angelina was standing on her bed doing curtsies.

When it was time for school, Angelina was trying on her mother's hats and making sad and funny faces at herself in the mirror. "You're going to be late again, Angelina!" cried Mrs Mouseling.

But Angelina did not care. She skipped over rocks

and practised high leaps over the flowerbeds until she landed in old

Mrs Hodgepodge's pansies and got a terrible scolding.

At playtime she twirled and spun across the playground so fast that none of the boys in her class could catch her and they were all very cross.

After school she did a beautiful arabesque in the kitchen and knocked over a jug of milk and a plate of her mother's best Cheddar cheese pies.

"Oh Angelina, your dancing is nothing but a
nuisance!" exclaimed her mother.

She sent Angelina straight upstairs to her room. Then Mrs Mouseling shook her head and said, "I just don't know what to do about Angelina." Mr Mouseling thought and then he said, "I think I may have an idea."

That same afternoon Mr and Mrs Mouseling went out together before the shops closed.

The next morning at breakfast Angelina found
a large box with her name on it.

Inside the box was a pink ballet dress and a pair of pink ballet slippers. Angelina's father smiled at her kindly. "I think you are ready to take ballet lessons," he said.

Angelina was so excited that she jumped straight up in the air and landed with one foot in her mother's sewing basket.

The very next day Angelina took her pink slippers
and ballet dress and went to her first lesson at
Miss Lilly's Ballet School. There were nine other
little girls in the class and they all practised curtsies
and pliés and ran around the room together just
like fairies. Then they skipped and twirled about
until it was time to go home.

"Congratulations, Angelina," said Miss Lilly,
"You are a good little dancer and
if you work hard you may grow
up to be a real ballerina one day."

Angelina ran all the way home to give her mother
a big hug. "I'm the happiest little girl in the world
today!" she said.

From that day on, Angelina came downstairs when her mother called her, she tidied her room, and she went to school on time.

She helped her mother
make Cheddar cheese pies

and she even let the boys catch her
in the playground sometimes.

Angelina went every day to her ballet lessons and
worked very hard for many years …
… until at last she became the famous ballerina,
Mademoiselle Angelina, and people came from
far and wide to enjoy her lovely dancing.